## Dear Parent:
## Your child's love of reading st

Every child learns to read in a different way and at his or her own speed. Some go back and forth between reading levels and read favorite books again and again. Others read through each level in order. You can help your young reader improve and become more confident by encouraging his or her own interests and abilities. From books your child reads with you to the first books he or she reads alone, there are I Can Read Books for every stage of reading:

### SHARED READING
Basic language, word repetition, and whimsical illustrations, ideal for sharing with your emergent reader

### BEGINNING READING
Short sentences, familiar words, and simple concepts for children eager to read on their own

### READING WITH HELP
Engaging stories, longer sentences, and language play for developing readers

### READING ALONE
Complex plots, challenging vocabulary, and high-interest topics for the independent reader

### ADVANCED READING
Short paragraphs, chapters, and exciting themes for the perfect bridge to chapter books

I Can Read Books have introduced children to the joy of reading since 1957. Featuring award-winning authors and illustrators and a fabulous cast of beloved characters, I Can Read Books set the standard for beginning readers.

A lifetime of discovery begins with the magical words "I Can Read!"

*Visit www.icanread.com for information*
*on enriching your child's reading experience.*

Spider-Man Versus Electro  © 2009 Marvel Entertainment, Inc., and its subsidiaries. MARVEL, all related characters and the distinctive likenesses thereof: ™ & © 2009 Marvel Entertainment, Inc., and its subsidiaries. Licensed by Marvel Characters B.V. www.marvel.com. All rights reserved. Printed in the United States of America. No part of this book may be used or reproduced in any manner whatsoever without written permission except in the case of brief quotations embodied in critical articles and reviews. For information address HarperCollins Children's Books, a division of HarperCollins Publishers, 10 East 53rd Street, New York, NY 10022.
www.icanread.com

Library of Congress catalog card number: 2008941560
ISBN 978-0-06-162621-0
Typography by John Sazaklis

12  13  LP/WOR  20  19  18  17  16    ❖    First Edition

# THE AMAZING SPIDER-MAN

## Spider-Man Versus Electro

By Susan Hill

Illustrations by MADA Design, Inc.

HarperCollins*Publishers*

## PETER PARKER

Peter Parker lives in New York City.

## FLASH THOMPSON

Peter goes to school with Flash Thompson. Flash isn't always very nice to him.

## ELECTRO

Electro is the newest villain in town. He can control the power of electricity.

## SPIDER-MAN

Peter has a secret identity.
He is Spider-Man!
He can walk on walls and shoot webs.

"Look out, bookworm!"

yelled Flash Thompson.

Flash threw a water balloon.

It hit Peter Parker on the head.

"I could be a bully like Flash if I used my amazing powers!" Peter said to himself. "Then I'd get some respect!"

"But I'm not a bully.
I'm Spider-Man,
and I use my powers for good,"
Peter said quietly as he walked.

Suddenly, the giant screen
in Times Square lit up.

A horrible face appeared.

"I am Electro,"

boomed a voice from the screen.

"All the power of electricity

is mine!" he said.

"With my electric rays I will put

the entire city in the dark.

Everyone will respect me!

Everyone will know my name!"

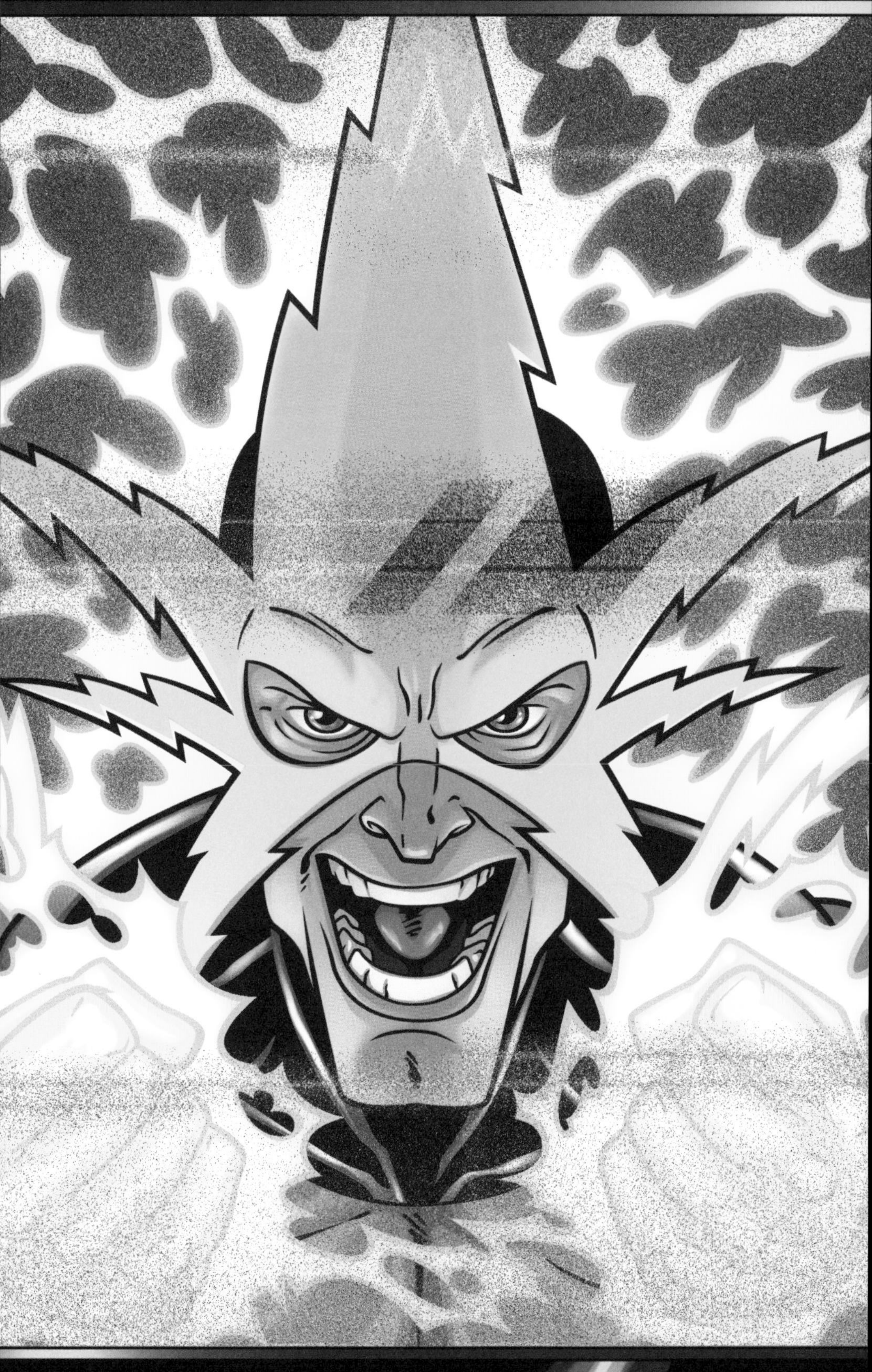

"What was that name again?" said Peter.

"Buzzy? Sparky?"

Electro spoke from his hideout.
"In five minutes,
the city will be dark.
Hospitals, schools, and jails,
all dark!" he said.

Peter knew what he had to do.

He put on his mask and suit.

He became Spider-Man!

"Electro must be at a power plant.

But which one?" said Spider-Man.

A police helicopter flew over.

"That was easy," said Spider-Man.

"Maybe I could get a ride!"

Spider-Man swung to the helicopter.

He was lifted high over the city.

Suddenly, the helicopter buzzed.

"We've been hit!" yelled the pilot.

"We've lost all power!"

Spider-Man quickly shot webs
to catch the helicopter.
"Thanks, Spider-Man!"
said the pilot.
"Anytime," said Spider-Man.
"But speaking of time,
I've got four minutes
to save the city!"

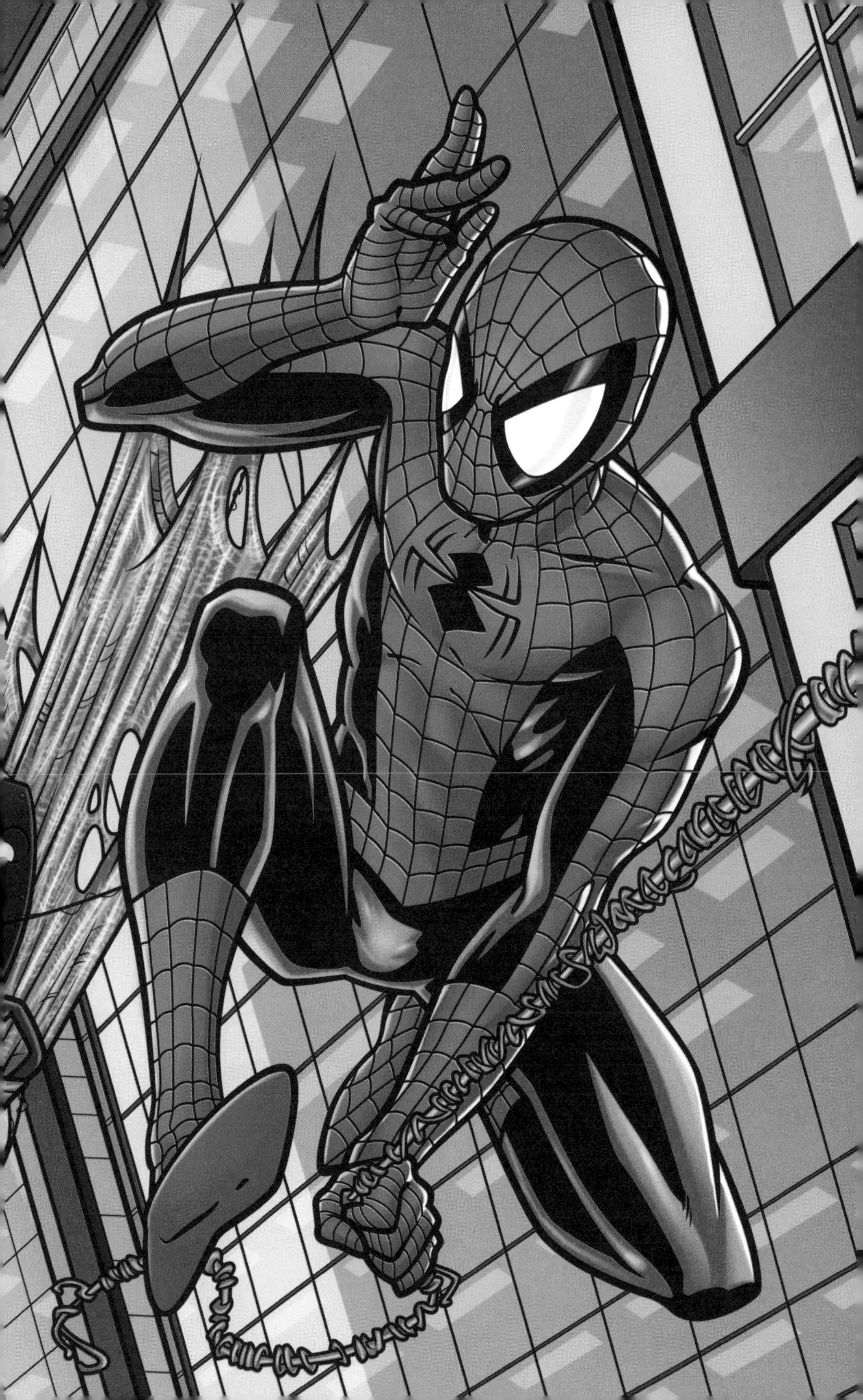

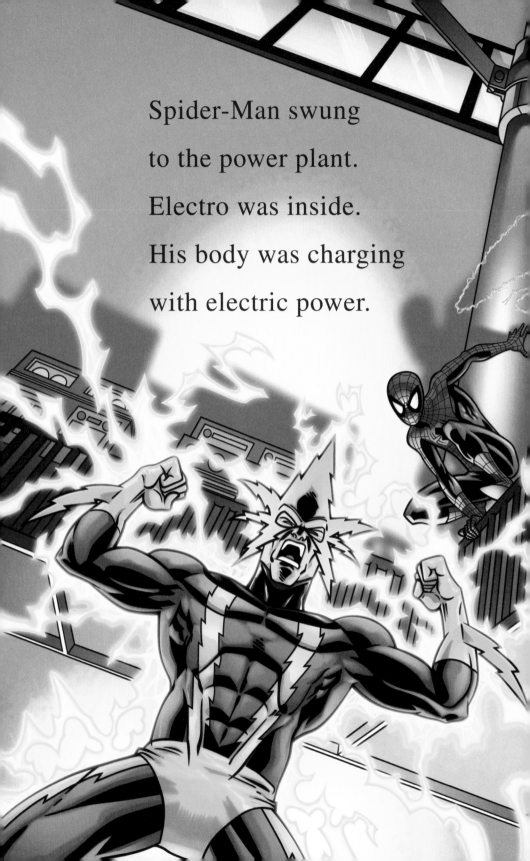

Spider-Man swung
to the power plant.
Electro was inside.
His body was charging
with electric power.

"Hey, Sparky!" shouted Spider-Man.

Electro turned and shot

a lightning bolt at Spider-Man.

"Don't call me Sparky!" he shouted.

"Missed me!" said Spider-Man.

Spidey hit Electro with a web.

*Pfffft!* The web sizzled to dust.

"Ha!" said Electro.

"Your powers are no good!

One touch of my electricity

and you'll fry!"

Spider-Man knew Electro was right.

How could he stop him?

Electro shot another bolt.

Spider-Man swung out of the way

just in time.

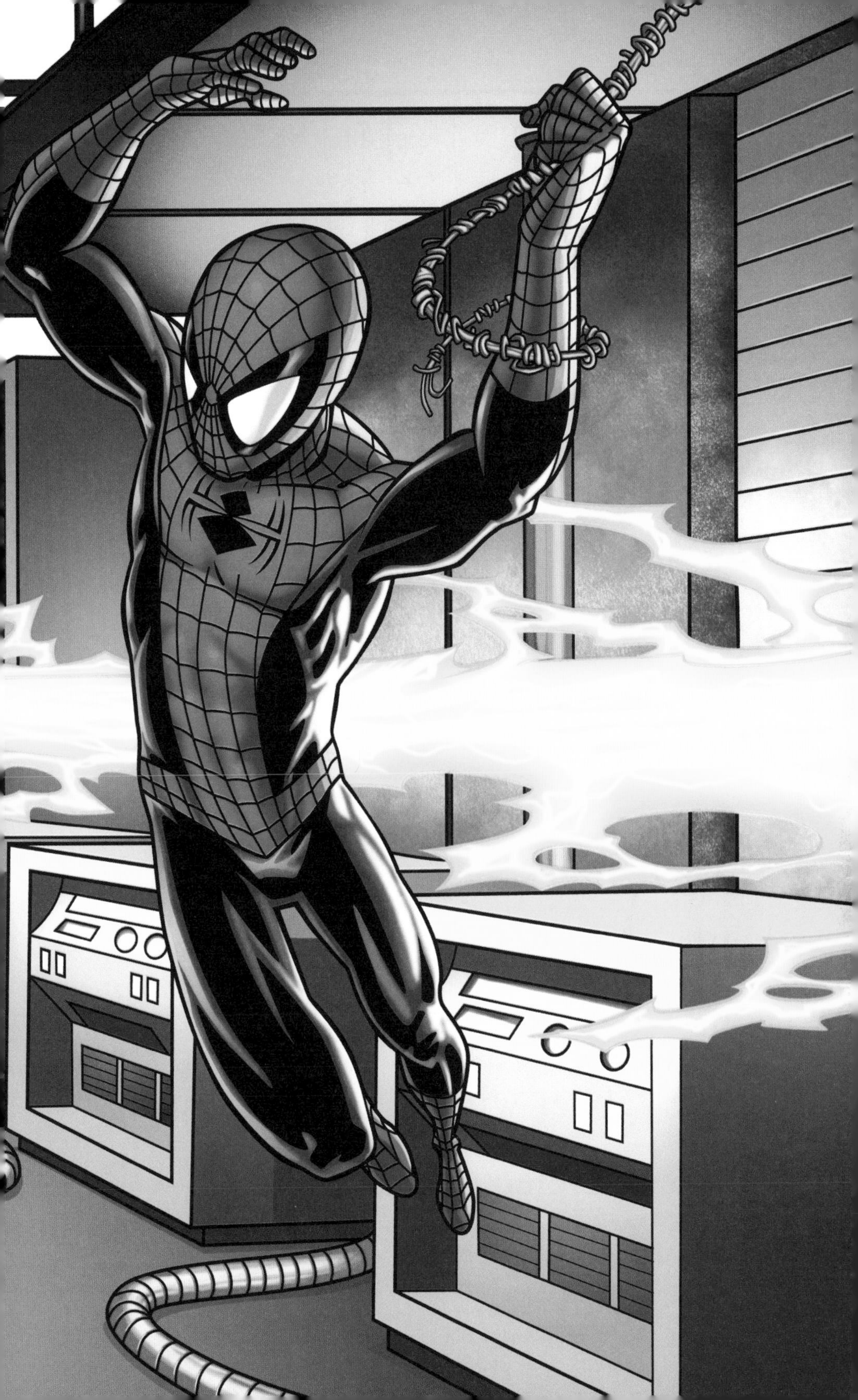

Then Spidey saw something helpful.
"The janitor won't mind if I borrow
his rubber gloves and boots."
The rubber will help protect me
from the electricity!" he said.

With the gloves on,

Spider-Man could knock Electro down.

But Electro shot back up

and sent Spider-Man flying!

"Ouch!" said Spider-Man.

He had crashed into a big pipe.

"Water!" he said.

"Why didn't I think of that?
Everyone knows mixing water
and electricity is very dangerous!"

Electro lifted his hands to shoot
one more bolt.

"Soon the city will be dark
and you'll show me some respect!"
he shouted.

"You don't get respect
by being a bully, Sparky!"
said Spider-Man.

Spidey turned on the water.

*Woosh!*

"It's lights-out for you, Electro!

Kids, don't try this at home!"

Electro fell to the floor.

"I've done it!" said Spider-Man.

"When Electro wakes up in jail,

it'll be the shock of his life!"